T0016934

SUPER
STICKER BOOK

A GOLDEN BOOK • NEW YORK

This book is based on the TV series Peppa Pig. Peppa Pig is created by Neville Astley and Mark Baker.
Peppa Pig © Astley Baker Davies Ltd/Entertainment One UK Ltd 2003.

www.peppapig.com

All rights reserved. Published in the United States by Golden Books, an imprint of Random House Children's Books, a division of Penguin Random House LLC, 1745 Broadway, New York, NY 10019, and in Canada by Penguin Random House Canada Limited, Toronto. Originally published in the United Kingdom by Parragon Books Ltd, Bath, in 2017.
Golden Books, A Golden Book, and the G colophon are registered trademarks of Penguin Random House LLC.

rhcbooks.com

ISBN 978-0-593-11893-1

MANUFACTURED IN CHINA

20 19 18 17 16 15 14

2019 Golden Books Edition

Playdate

Peppa and Suzy are having a playdate. Find and circle three things that are different in the second picture.

Answers on page 63

To the Henhouse

Help Peppa reach Granny Pig's henhouse so she can see if there are eggs to collect.

Start

Finish

Answer on page 63

Time for Class

Draw a small arrow pointing to the 9 and a big arrow pointing to the 12 on the clock in Madame Gazelle's classroom. Then circle the number in the window that tells you what time it is.

Answers on page 63

Robot George

George loves to dress up as a robot. Find and circle the one picture of Robot George that is different from the rest.

Muddy Path

Which path will get Candy to Danny so they can splash and play in the mud puddle?

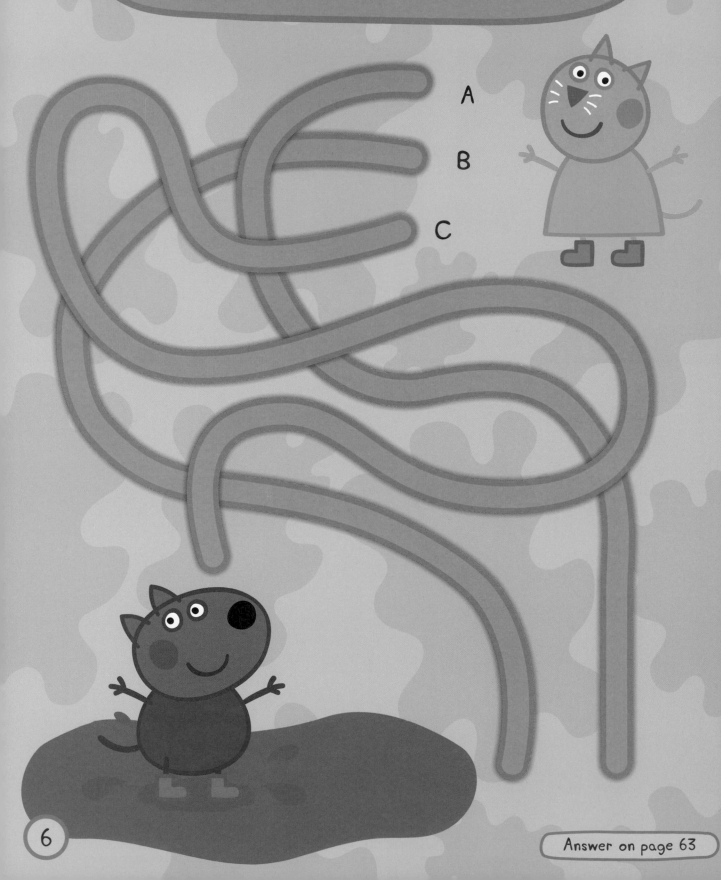

A

B

C

6

Answer on page 63

Laugh Lines

How many laughing friends are in each line below? Put the number in the circle, and draw a smiley face next to the line with the most friends.

A Special Visitor

Connect the dots to see who visits Peppa when Peppa is fast asleep after she loses her first tooth.

Answer on page 63

Bedtime Buddies

Draw lines to connect Peppa and George with their own special bedtime buddy.

A Ducky Picnic

How many ducks have come to Peppa's family picnic?
Circle the correct number.

Answer on page 63

Pedaling Pals

Peppa is ready for a bike ride with Suzy. How fast can you get her through the maze to her friend?

Start

Finish

Pizza Party!

Draw a line between each plate and a member of Peppa's family. Are there enough plates so everyone can have a slice of pizza?

Answer on page 63

A Flower for Peppa

Peppa painted a pretty flower for you.
Can you draw one for her?

Muddy Puddle Huddle

Everyone loves jumping in muddy puddles! Can you find three things that are different in the second picture?

Answers on page 63

Ask an adult to cut this out.

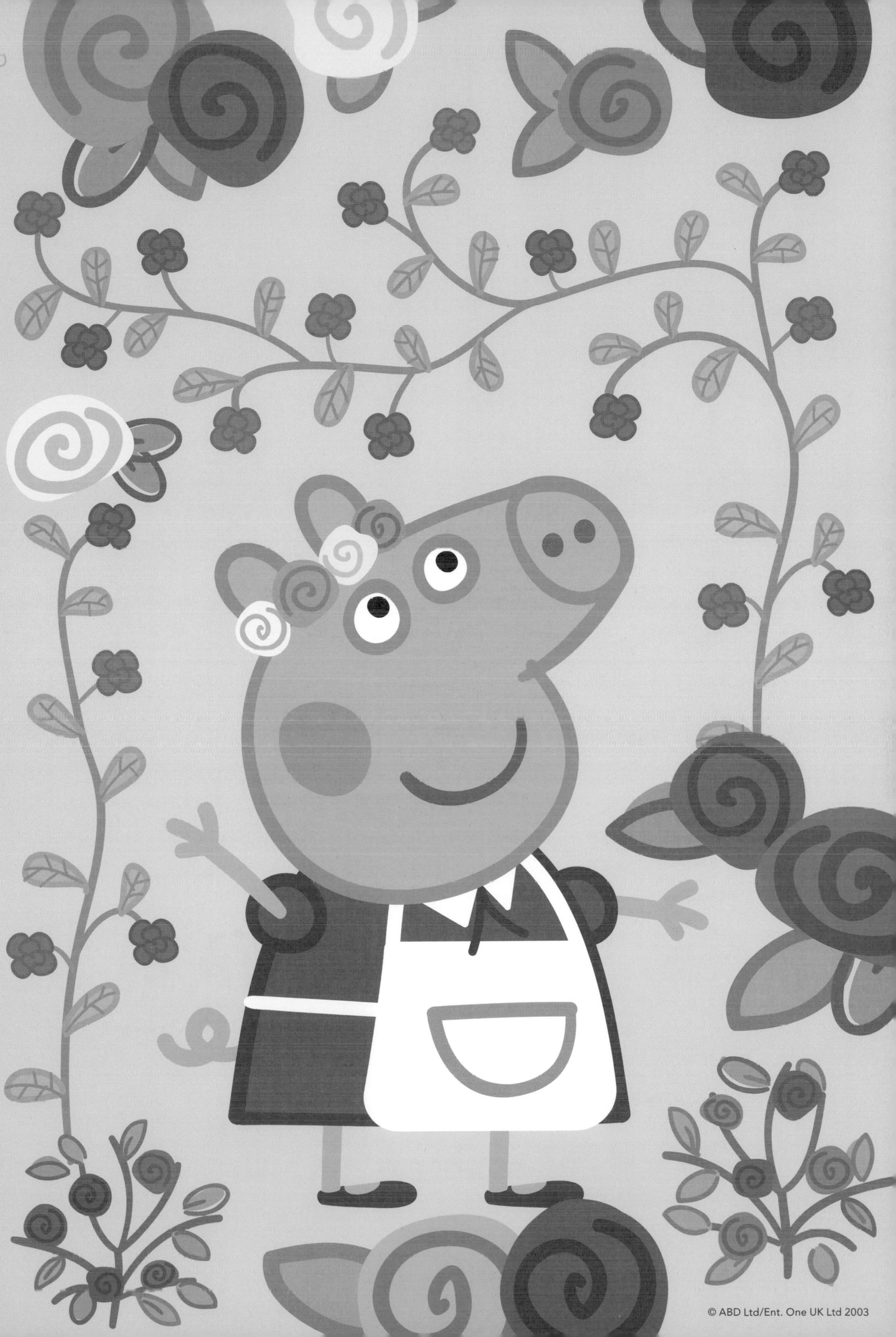

The Flyaway Kite

The kite's string broke, and the wind blew the kite away from Peppa and her family. Draw a new string from Daddy Pig's hand to the kite so they can get the kite out of the tree.

Buzz! Buzz!

Peppa is a busy bee. Count the number
of her bee friends in each row.

Answers on page 63

Take a Look Around

Everyone in Madame Gazelle's class is looking around for something to paint. Can you see where each of these close-ups belongs in the bigger picture? Draw a line to each one that you can find.

Answers on page 63

Giant Mud Puddle

Draw the giant mud puddle that Peppa, Suzy, and George just splashed around in!

Pretty New Shoes

Look at Peppa's new, pretty red shoes!

Circle all the blue shoes and boots you see.
Put a check mark on all the yellow ones.
Add a dot to all the purple ones.
What other color shoes do you see?

Answers on page 63

Happy Little Tigers

Draw a line between each tiger and who they really are underneath the face paint.

Answers on page 63

Warm Friends

Help Peppa and Danny Dog through the maze to reach the snowman. They want to give him a carrot nose.

Start

Finish

Answer on page 63

Treasure Hunt

Peppa and George have a map that shows them where treasure is buried. Draw what you think they will find.

What's Her Name?

This friend of Peppa's loves to play with building blocks. Can you fill in the letters of her name on the building blocks below? Pick the letters from the clue box.

E _ _ _ _ Y

CLUE BOX

L   I   M

Answer on page 63

Surprise, Mummy!

Peppa, George, and Daddy surprise Mummy with breakfast in bed. Can you find and circle three things that are different in the second picture?

Answers on page 63

Sheriff Pedro

Trace over the lines to give Sheriff Pedro a star on his hat and one on his vest, too.

Zoe Loves Playgroup

Help get Zoe up the hill to playgroup—
she can't wait to get there!

Finish

Start

Answer on page 64

A Balloon for George

Draw a circle around the balloon you
think George would want. Then draw a
heart around the one you want.

Busy Boys

Edmond, Richard, and George are
very busy with their trucks.

Draw a circle around the red truck.
Put a check mark next to the orange truck.
Draw a square around the yellow truck.

Answers on page 64

The Rabbit Family's Home

Draw a square around each window you see in Rebecca Rabbit's burrow.

Bedtime Snack

Yum, yum! George loves his bedtime snack.
Draw what he is eating.

It's a Match

Draw a line between each character
and their shadow.

Answers on page 64

Rebecca's Favorite Food

Rebecca Rabbit is dressed as her favorite food.
Use the code below to find out what it is.

A C O R T
1 2 3 4 5

— — — — — — —
1 2 1 4 4 3 5

Answer on page 64

Where Is Mr. Dinosaur?

It's almost time for bed, but George can't find Mr. Dinosaur! Can you circle Mr. Dinosaur in the picture?

Answer on page 64

Elegant Emily

Find and circle the image of Emily Elephant that doesn't match the rest.

Answer on page 64

Grandpa's Garden

Follow the tasty fruits and vegetables to get Peppa to Grandpa Pig in his garden.

Answer on page 64

Noisy Friends!

Draw a line between each of Peppa's friends and the sound they make.

Meow

Woof

Yap

Baa

Answers on page 64

Helping Mummy Work

Match up the pieces to complete the picture so Peppa and George can help Mummy do her work.

1 **2** **3**

To the Supermarket

Help the Pig family get to the supermarket so they can buy some yummy food.

Finish

Start

Answer on page 64

Fun at the Playground

Draw a line between each character who has a little brother with her at the playground. Then circle the total number of characters you drew lines between.

In the Kitchen

Find and put a check mark on these shapes in Peppa's kitchen:

54

Answers on page 64

Swimming Along

Which path will get George over to Peppa so they can swim together?

A   B   C

Mail Delivery

Connect the dots so Zoe Zebra can help her father deliver the mail.

Answer on page 64

Fun at the Fair

Everyone is having fun at the fair. Put a check mark next to each close-up of Peppa's friends and family when you find them in the bigger picture.

Big Red Apples

How many big red apples are on the
tree in Grandpa Pig's garden?

Answer on page 64

A Present for Peppa

Draw what you think is inside the box.

Birthday Balloons

It's Mummy's birthday!
Say "Happy Birthday, Mummy Pig!"

How many blue balloons do you see? _____

How many green balloons do you see? _____

How many pink balloons do you see? _____

How many yellow balloons do you see? _____

How many orange balloons do you see? _____

Answers on page 64

Answers

Page 2

Page 3

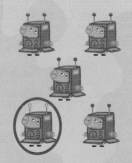

Page 4

 9

Page 5

Page 6 - Path C

Page 9 - 5, 4, 2
The first line has the most friends.

Page 10 - the tooth fairy

Page 11

Page 12 - 3 ducks

Page 15

Page 16 - Yes. There are 6 members of Peppa's family and 6 plates with pizza.

Page 18

Page 22 - 4, 3, 2

Page 23

Page 27

There are also orange and green shoes.

Page 28

Page 29

Page 31 - E M I L Y

Page 32

63

Answers

Page 34

Page 36

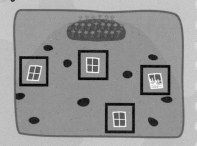

Page 39

Page 41

Page 42 – A CARROT

Page 45

Page 46

Page 47

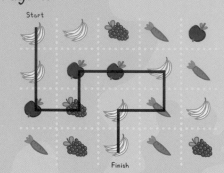

Page 48

Page 51 – 1. B
2. C
3. A

Page 52

Page 53

Page 54

Page 57 – Path C

Page 58

Page 59

Page 60 – 9 apples

Page 62 – 2, 2, 2, 3, 3